This Book
Belongs To:

....

....

Bedtime Stories

Bedtime
Stories

Bath • New York • Singapore • Hong Kong • Cologne • Delhi
Melbourne • Amsterdam • Johannesburg • Auckland • Shenzhen

Illustrated by Alison Atkins

This edition published by Parragon in 2011

Parragon
Queen Street House
4 Queen Street
Bath BA1 1HE, UK

ISBN 978-1-4454-1979-4

Printed in China

Contents

Teddy Goes Flying

Every day, Teddy played in the garden with Jamie.

One morning, Jamie accidentally dropped Teddy into a puddle. Jamie went rushing indoors to tell Mum.

"Don't worry, Jamie," said Mum. "We'll put Teddy in the washing machine with the towels. He'll soon be clean again."

Teddy went round and round in the washing machine. The soap bubbles washed out all the mud. Soon Teddy was nice and clean.

Swish, swish, swish!

Then Mum hung Teddy out to dry on the washing line while she and Jamie went shopping.

Suddenly, the wind blew Teddy off the line.

Teddy swept and swooped over rooftops and gardens. He soared, glided, dipped and flipped. He had never had so much fun!

"Whee!" Teddy called. "I'm flying!"

Teddy flew down over one garden where there were swings and a slide and a big climbing-frame.

"What fun Jamie and I could have playing there!" he thought.

Suddenly, the wind started to drop. Teddy fell all the way down to the ground, and…**SPLASH!** into another big puddle, right in front of Jamie's house.

"It's Teddy!" cried Jamie, running ahead as they returned home. "He's wet and muddy again!"

"We'll have to pop him back into the washing machine," said Mum.

Suddenly the wind picked up.

"Only this time," she added, "I think we'll let him dry in the airing cupboard!"

"Good idea," said Jamie.

"A very good idea!" thought Teddy.

Ben's Boots

Ben really loved his shiny blue boots. When it rained, he would **splash** in the puddles on his way to nursery.

Even when it was hot, Ben would wear his blue boots!

One morning Ben found it hard to put his boots on. Mum said he should have some new ones as he'd grown too big for them.

"I don't want new ones," said Ben at once.

"You can't wear boots that are too small, Ben," said Mum. "They'll hurt your feet."

The lady at the shoe shop didn't have any blue boots in Ben's size.

"You'll have to try these yellow ones on, Ben," Mum said. "They look really good."

"No they don't!" thought Ben. "I won't wear them!"

At home,
Ben tugged and
pulled his old
boots on. Then he
went into the kitchen
for tea. Mum saw the
boots, and smiled.

"Okay," she said.
"You can wear your
blue boots for
one last time."

Ben wore
them all through
story time after tea.

"Right, Ben," Mum said,
as she closed the book. "It's time for bed,
and you can't wear
boots in bed."

"Yes I can,"
said Ben, running
up the stairs
and jumping
into bed.

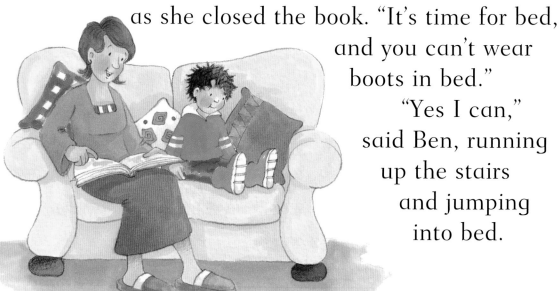

Ben grabbed his favourite teddy and held him tight.

And that was when Mum had an idea.

"Poor Ted," she said. "I thought he could have your blue boots, Ben, so he could come out with you to play when it's wet."

"Oh!" said Ben. This was really difficult. He couldn't keep his old boots if Ted needed them, could he? And it would be great to take Ted out in the rain with him.

Ben tugged off his blue boots. He slipped them onto Ted's feet.

Mum handed the yellow boots to Ben. He slipped them on and lifted his feet up to show Ted.

"Ben's boots!" he said proudly.

Jack and the Mice

Jack was Katy Cat's kitten.

"I'm going to teach you about mice," Katy Cat said to Jack. "It's our job to catch them."

Jack liked catching things, so this sounded fun.

At the other end of the garden, Mitzi Mouse and her children, Miles and Melanie, came out of their nest.

"I want you to look for food," she told them, "but you must watch out for cats!"

"What's a cat?" asked Miles and Melanie together.

"Cats are very dangerous creatures," their mother explained. "They move very fast, but you must move faster!"

Miles and Melanie both nodded. "We will, Mum," they promised.

A little while later, Jack was sniffing all around and twitching his whiskers as he looked around for mice.

Not far away, Miles and Melanie went out to look for food, with their whiskers wiggling and their tails twittering.

Jack saw the two little creatures running through the grass.

"Are you mice?" Jack asked them.

"Y-yes," said Miles, nervously.

"Are you a cat?" asked Melanie.

"Yes," said Jack. "I think I'm supposed to catch you, but I'd rather play."

So Jack and Miles and Melanie began to play together.

The three friends were right in the middle of a wonderful game of tag when Katy Cat looked up and saw Jack chasing Miles and Melanie.

At that moment, Mitzi Mouse came out of her nest and saw her children running away from Jack.

As Miles and Melanie ran away, Jack padded back to his mum, who was pleased to see him chasing mice.

And on the other side of the garden, Mitzi Mouse was glad to see her children escape from the cat.

Jack looked back at Miles and Melanie.

All three winked, then gave a little wave with their tails and twitched their whiskers. It was their way of letting each other know they'd be back again tomorrow – to have lots more fun together!

Backstroke Benny

Mama Duck looked at her four new ducklings, Benny, Kenny, Jenny and Penny. She wanted them to become strong swimmers, so the ducklings practised flapping their feet every day.

"Get ready for your first swim, my dears!" she told her ducklings one day. "Line up behind me."

"Now," said Mama Duck, when everyone was in the water, "stay right behind me, flap your feet, and –

SWIM!"

The little ducklings followed behind Mama Duck – all except Benny, who was going the wrong way!

"You're doing the backstroke," called Mama Duck. "You need to flap your feet forward!"

Benny tried to flap his feet forward, but they wouldn't go. He just went backwards faster.

"It's no use!" he called. "I can only swim backwards!"

Benny's family tried to help, but no matter what they did, Benny could only swim one way – backwards!

As they swam along the lake, Jenny, Penny and Kenny told Benny what they could see up ahead, and Benny told them what he could see happening behind them.

"A fox is coming out of the trees and two rabbits are running away," said Benny.

"A fox?" said his brother and sisters.

"A FOX!" quacked Mama Duck. "Quick! We have to get away!"

"Follow me!" said Benny, swimming to the front of the line. Doing the backstroke, Benny guided his family away from the fox.

When the fox was gone, everyone breathed a sigh of relief. Then they gathered round Benny.

"Benny, your backstroke saved the day," said Mama Duck. "Three cheers for Backstroke Benny!"

As everyone cheered, Mama Duck watched proudly.

"I knew all my ducklings would be fine swimmers," she thought, "but even I didn't know just how special Backstroke Benny would be!"

Jasmine's Summer Lullaby

One warm summer's night, Jasmine just could not get to sleep. The next day was her birthday and she was very excited.

"What I really need is someone to sing me a lullaby," she muttered to herself.

A small bird outside Jasmine's bedroom window heard this and sang to her. Then her cat and dog tried to join in!

But it didn't make Jasmine sleepy.

Soon, Mum came in to see what all the noise was about.

"I can't sleep," said Jasmine.

"Well, I'll sing you the lullaby my mother sang to me," said Mum. "It always sent me to sleep."

Jasmine snuggled up against her mum to listen.

Mum gently began to sing a soft lullaby. Soon, all the animals began to join in with her mother's singing.

The sound was so restful that in no time at all Jasmine was fast asleep. ZZZZZZZZZZZ!

Her mother quietly stopped singing, and tucked the covers around Jasmine's chin. She then put a little present on the pillow by Jasmine's head.

"Something for you to open when you wake up, Jasmine," she whispered. "Now, come along you animals, time for us all to go to sleep."

Soon all of the animals had dozed off happily too.

In the morning, Jasmine spotted the present Mum had left on her pillow.

"Ooh, a birthday present!" she cried, unwrapping it excitedly. Inside the bright wrapping paper was a little musical box. When Jasmine opened the lid, the box played the tune that her mother had sung to her the night before.

"Now I can to get to sleep whenever I want to," said Jasmine happily and, from then on, she always could.